BABA'S REMINISCENCE

BY

PRITI MOHANTY

ISBN 978-93-5458-095-6

© Priti Mohanty 2021

Published in India 2020 by Pencil

A brand of

One Point Six Technologies Pvt. Ltd.

123, Building J2, Shram Seva Premises,

Wadala Truck Terminal, Wadala (E)

Mumbai 400037, Maharashtra, INDIA

E connect@thepencilapp.com

W www.thepencilapp.com

DISCLAIMER: *The opinions expressed in this book are those of the authors and do not purport to reflect the views of the Publisher.*

AUTHOR BIOGRAPHY

<u>**Writing and Compiling by :-**</u>

PRITIMOHANTY

- She has stepped into the world of writing as a storyteller as well as a poet.

- she has worked in 12 anthologies as a co-writer.

- This is her first solo work.

<u>**Concept by :-**</u>

ASUTOSHMOHANTY

- He has a keen interest in literature.

- He has worked as an article and report writer.

- His love for Sai baba made him think about this wonderful initiative

CONTENTS

ACKNOWLEDGEMENTS

We offer our sincere gratitude to Ganapati, whose blessings are the first and foremost before initiating something.

Maa saraswati, the Goddess of knowledge who helped us to beautify our book with the ornaments of words.

Our prime deity lord Jagannath for providing the strength and support to complete this task successfully.

Our spiritual master as well as our sadguru SAI BABA who is the key reason of this book. And without his willingness and blessings this wouldn't have been possible at all.

At the end a special thanks to our living Gods, our parents who stood behind us a pillars and helped us take forward this work ahead.

Thanking each and every person who devoted their valuable time in sharing their experiences with us.

SAI – A SYNONYM OF MIRACLE

Baba's charismatic deeds dragged me towards himself when I was at a very young age. I get an internal satisfaction when I started worshipping him.

One morning when I was staying in Bhubaneswar during my class 11th, I was on the way to my school, I was late by 10 minutes so I was in a hurry. When I was passing through a traffic, the place named sisubhavan square in Bhubaneswar,

I saw a person with a white kaftan with his head covered with a white cloth, he had white beard and was holding a Jholi kind of a bag and he was in bare foots. He was walking vigorously in search of someone, his face seemed to be a bit stressed. The moment he cross passed me I got goosebumps. I just stopped my vehicle, folded my hands and I bowed down and I was just wondering that why people are not noticing him.

Is he really Baba who is walking down in this road ?

I still remember how he looked, the way he covered his head with white cloth the way he walked. I don't know but I just felt like Baba cross passed me. I can never forget that moment in my life.

Secondly, December of the year 2019 was the most painful phase of my life.

On December 20 my pre board exams got over so I came home. On December 22, I went to Barbati Stadium with my siblings to watch India match for the first time in my life and what happened was that I lost my phone there.

It definitely disappointed me a lot.

On 24 December which was my birthday, my mother got admitted in hospital because she suffered from a brain stroke. On 24th evening when I went to see her in the ICU she couldn't utter a single word. She was trying to say me so many things but she couldn't.

That was the most devastating and depressing moment in my life. I never thought that I will face such a difficult situation in my life and that too on my birthday. I came out, I asked Baba "what mistake I did ?" I never think bad of anyone. I have always believed your sayings that is "SERVICE TO MANKIND IS SERVICE TO GOD ". Then what kind of a gift you gave me in my birthday ? Is this genuine baba ? PLease answer me".

On the very next day, the doctor said me that your mother is improving, when I went inside she could talk to me and you all will be surprised to know that within just a week on the 1st of January she was completely alright I think that was all possible only because of Baba's grace and nothing else.

Its wrong that baba doesn't give any kind of pain or difficulties to his devotees, he takes even more exams of his devotees than other people but he always gives us the strength to fight with that and he always has some lessons to teach us with his tests.

I feel really grateful to Baba that he gave me this opportunity to compile this book. I had never thought of in my dreams that I will start my work with this.

Baba, I need you not only in my failure, but in my success too.

Baba, I want you not only in my valleys, but in my peaks too.

Baba, I love you not only when I need you, but when you need me too.

Omm Sai Ram
PRITI MOHANTY
CUTTACK ODISHA

BOW TO SHREE SAI, PEACE BE TO ALL

BABA -
A RELIEF FROM ALL PAIN

I didn't have a strong belief on Sai Baba, untill one of my friend from US made me know about him. They used to visit India once a year just to pay homage to Shirdi Sai Baba. Then once I started worshipping him, I found that he is a rock solid who is always present in our ups, downs, good and bad.

Once I visited Shirdi. While returning from the hall of Baba after darshan we get a packet of prasadam and a packet of udi. When I got mine I was coming forward but suddenly a person tapped on my shoulder and said, "I haven't got my Udi can you please ask them to give me one ". When I asked them they said "the one who has walked out this way can't get another, you have to make another Darshan to get another udi "he was disappointed so what I did was that I gave my udi to him.

I felt a bit bad that I couldn't get one for myself when I came out and I saw my husband and son standing, my husband said me "Mini, I don't know how but mistakenly I got two udi packets". I was completely dumbstruck and thought how could this happen. This was an unforgettable moment in my life.

Not only this I feel Baba's miracles in each step of my life.

When my son was preparing for JEE we were a bit worried that if the percentage of boards were considered then he might not crack the exam. I always prayed Baba to help me out and to our amazement, the year when my son appeared JEE, class 12 percentage was ruled out to be taken into consideration so my son could successfully clear the exam.

I can't thank baba much for this. These magical deeds are only possible in his Behalf.

Omm Sai Ram
MINI MITRA
KOLKATA

BOW TO SHREE SAI, PEACE BE TO ALL

SAI –
A COMPANION OF SORROW

I feel the presence of Baba in each and every day of my life. I came in contact with his miraculous deeds when I was at a very young age. When I was just 13 or 14 years old me and a friend of mine decided to visit Shirdi together. In total we both had nearly about 5,000 rupees with us but since we were very young, we were very curious to explore even more than what we hadplanned.

We Started our journey from Kharagpur then we went to Visakhapatnam then we had planned to visit Tirupati and then Shirdi.

When we reached Pune we were completely out of money, we had only rupees 200 left with us which wasn't even enough for us to get shelter somewhere. When we got a place to stay for a night, we met a person from Mumbai who was a highly established businessman. At night when we shared our situation with that person he lent his hand forward for helping us.

At that particular moment when we didn't have enough money with us we even thought of stealing it from that person who seem to be a well-to-do man but that person turned out to be so good that he took us everywhere he went, every place he visited, to every good hotels he used to have his food. The the way he treated us, I would never hesitate comparing him with Baba. I just felt like it was Baba himself who helped us without any expectation of getting anything in return.

Secondly in this last year 2020 the whole world suffered badly from the deadly disease Corona. That hit me hard too. My situation was so terrible that no hopes were left with me than leaving it on Baba.

I was not only admitted to the hospital but was placed in the ICU for 2 to 3 days which affected my complete body but the only ray of hope which I had was Baba's miracle and the only thing which I used to overcome that deadly situation was Baba's UDI. Even I don't know how I got rescued from that situation, it was only Baba who holded my hand and brought me here to a normal life once again.

Omm Sai Ram
SOMNATH SHARMA
CUTTACK, ODISHA

BOW TO SHREE SAI, PEACE BE TO ALL

LIFE – A VOID WITHOUT SAI

I currently finished my Ph.D. studies successfully. It's happened due to our Sai. Without him, I wouldn't be completing it. From starting, my Ph.D. journey was hard. Every step was challenging until I lost my confidence and was in dilemma to complete my studies. There was a stage where the machine I was dealing with got repaired and we have to send it overseas.

I was blamed for not taking care of it properly (it may be my mistake too). The money needed for the repair was huge where my supervisor turned bitter as we have to use our own grant money. My work was also got stalled for one year plus. I was in depression. But with Sai's blessings, our school management agreed to repair it using their fund.

There are few times I felt my seniors and even my supervisor pressured me to the max. I still remember sitting in the lab until early morning, crying and asking mental strength from Sai. Sai was there for me. He made to be strong and helped me to face the hurdles.

There was another big help from Sai. I was rushing in sending my thesis draft until I made a small mistake but it was pretty obvious. I realized the mistake and corrected it during the viva exam. But none of the examiners questioned the mistake I did and surprisingly all of them praised my works. Yeah, it was a long period for me to complete my Ph.D. (It took almost 5 years plus) but without Sai guidance, I don't think I can complete it. Thank you Sai for helping me go through this.

Omm Sai Ram
SEETHA MUNISAMI
MALAYSIA

BOW TO SHREE SAI, PEACE BE TO ALL

BABA - RIVER OF PEACE

In the name of Sai, I would first like to bow down and present my gratitude tohim.

I never suffered from any diseases, neither diabetes nor thyroid. In 2017, I was diagnosed with breast cancer. I used to worship him from him a long time. I always asked him how could you give me such a big disease after I am your devotee and I worship you with all my heart and mind.

He came to my dream and said "why are you thinking so much, don't worry I am always there with you."

I had to undergo an operation and eventually I got well. And I could lead a normal lifestyle now.

And only because of his blessings and miraculous deeds I got rescued from such a deadly disease like cancer.

He is the lord of lords, may every creature stay blessed with his mesmerizing powers.

OMM SAI RAM
JHARANA PARIDA
CUTTACK, ODISHA

BOW TO SHREE SAI, PEACE BE TO ALL

BABA –
CAME FOR ALMS

I bow to Shree Sai, who is bliss incarnate.

It is an incident of year 2005, when on a Thursday, my mother was preparing afternoon meals. My mother used to fast on Thursdays and prepared naivedya for Baba. In the noon time, after performing Baba's worship with all due formalities, all of us partook Baba's prasad as meal.

As my mother was deeply engrossed in her domestic chores, a fakir wearing a white kafni and carrying a zoli around his shoulder acme at our doorstep. His characteristics resembled to Baba. My mother addressed him as "Baba". She immediately rushed to the cooking place and took three packets. She made a separate packet of uncooked rice, another packet consisting lentils and a distinct packet with a few vegetables. As she was preparing all these donations, the omniscient Baba, standing on the doorstep said, "O Maa! Give me the items separately. Everyone gives me food mixed together in a packet. I need to sort the rice and lentils separately before cooking them." The kitchen was in the opposite direction from the threshold where he stood.

My mother immediately went out with the food items and told, "Baba! I have placed all the items separately." He immediately accepted the donation. He took out a packet from his Zoli after keeping the food, and showed the zoli to my mother. There was a plastic packet that contained a mixture of cheap quality rice and lentils, filled with bugs, and said, "see, how people give me alms. But you are so generous Maa!"

Every Thursday, my mother used to cook surplus food for distribution to the poor children in our neighbourhood. And my father fed stray dogs everyday. My mother had narrated everything that had happened, over the lunch plate, my father was delighted to hear about the fakir. The seeds of devotion had already started sprouting deep inside his heart.

After we had completed eating our food, the leftover food was being served to dogs, by my father. The main road was visible from the long and narrow lane from where the hungry dogs came running. My father upturned the contents of the plate on a clean cement slab, where the food was regularly served. As he turned, after giving the food, to his great surprize, he saw the fakir standing behind him and watching his actions. My father started wandering, as to how was it possible for such an old man to walk the long distance within a time period of less than even ten seconds?

The fakir commented, "Babu! Do not feed the dogs on the open concrete slab. Try to feed them on a mud vessel. My father immediately rushed to a nearby sweet shop and brought a mud vessel for feeding the dogs. He kept it at a corner of the concrete slab and smiled looking at the fakir, for such a beautiful advice. As my father started to make a diligent search inside his pocket for offering dakshina, the fakir said, "Maa has beautifully given me things to eat. Now I shall return and cook some plateable food for my consumption."

Saying these lines, he disappeared. my father was astonished to see such a sight. He made a diligent search all around. He asked various people whether they had seen any fakir coming out from the lane. None gave a positive reply. Nor did he go to any neighbouring house for begging alms. We all believed, that the fakir was indeed Baba, who came to our house, making it his temple, by coming and standing there. We felt ourselves very lucky that Baba's footsteps touched our doorstep. Let me now conclude this chapter, putting into play my memories, imagining the divine look of Baba taking away all our sins by begging als, and advising us beautifully to offer meals to hungry dogs in an earthen pot.

Omm sai ram
PRITAM GHOSH
KOLKATA

BOW TO SHREE SAI, PEACE BE TO ALL

SAI - ANTAGONIST TO SUFFERINGS

Although I remain inclined to Jagannath, I always believe baba's powers and worship him.

When my elder sister was 5 months pregnant, the baby was miscarriaged. Although everyone knew that she had to face a stillbirth but the problem was that, it was very difficult to bring the baby out. The doctors were trying very hard but were failed repeatedly.

That day I went to baba's temple and gave the pandit ghee for starting a akhand diya. The moment I came home I heard that the baby is successfully taken out and my sister is alright now.

I heaved a sigh of relief and I thanked baba for this unbelievable miracle.

Worshipping him gives me an eternal peace which I love and due to that reason I always do Sai guruwar vrat. His blessings are with each and every soul irrationally who believe him and try to reach him.

Omm Sai Ram
PUJA MOHANTY
CUTTACK, ODISHA

BOW TO SHREE SAI, PEACE BE TO ALL

FAITH – ANOTHER NAME OF SAI

'Sai' the name of a blissful ocean, where one can rinse all his sorrows, depression, anxieties and come out with a heavenly peace. He always said to practice a simple but strong thing that is 'faith'.

Whenever I read Sai Satcharitra it again and again incandescent the inarticulate situation of my life.

The armaments required to overcome any situation that are reverence and endurance when added gives out 'Faith'.

One night my 7 years old daughter had a very highly temperature. Her body was burning up with fever. My husband and I tried to lower it down in many ways but we failed. The darkness of the night and the rising temperature made me helpless and feel suffocated. A helpless mother sat near her sick baby with tears in her eyes.

We had a photo of Sai baba in that room. My teary eyes looked at baba and a serious conversation started. All the doctors are asleep but the great doctor of the world is awaken for 24/7. Yes, all the medicine stores were closed but the Sanjivani of this world is with you. That is the small package of miracle- Udi of Baba.

It did its magic within minutes and the temperature came lowered in lesser time than any other paracetamol medicines. This process kept continuing till 5 am.

Though I couldn't get any permanent or fruitful results my faith didn't decrease. I again started saying him. "No, I am not the mother of my baby, I am rather a caretaker of your baby. You have appointed me to take care of your ansh (part). I only do my duty but the responsibility is your.

At 5.30 a voice of anger within me said baba baba if the temperature doesn't comes down entirety then I will have to stop the application of udi or in other words have to stop the flow of my faith on you. But this time a miracle happened the last application of udi threw out the temperature.

What I learned that only our faith makes us powerful and makes the situation powerless.

Because 'faith' is another situation of 'Sai'.

Omm Sai Ram
SWEEKRUTI MOHANTY
CUTTACK, ODISHA

BOW TO SHREE SAI, PEACE BE TO ALL

BABA-
A BARRIER TO ALL OBSTACLES

Since last 20-25 years me and family have taken shelter under the blessed tree of Sai baba. Baba more or less has always been there with us in every ups and downs ofmine.

In this last December, the marriage of my son was finalized. All arrangements were done and the date was also decided which was December 11. On the day of marriage, since the bride's house was a bit far away from our place so we had to be in a hurry to reach there. Just after 30 minutes of the journey from our home, a bike came and hit my son's car.

Just within a blink of Eyes our car went through small shops thereby and suddenly stopped. it's only because of Baba's blessings that he saved my son and the other two people who were there in the car, from such a big accident.

My son was a bit sad that it was the first day of his new life and this is what happened with him.The driver went and got another car and all of them went through that car.

I always prayed since a long time that baba please take care of everything and make everything possible peacefully and successfully.

Finally all the rituals were done and both my son and daughter-in-law returned home safely. One of the biggest thing is that the daughter-in-law which we got is beautiful, calm, composed and a very good care taker.

I just pray Baba to keep showering his love and blessings over my family members forever.

We would always be indebted to him.

Omm Sai Ram

BHARTI PATTANAIK

TITLAGARH, ODISHA

BOW TO SHREE SAI, PEACE BE TO ALL

BABA REMEMBERS EVERY PROMISE

I have numerous experiences with Baba. His role in my life is completelydivine.

When my elder son was about to appear his 10th exams he was the little bit weak in Social Studies. I used to pray Baba a lot. I used to go with him till examination centre, drop him and come back start doing Baba's parayan and due too Baba's Grace he could secure very good marks and pass with CGPA 10.

My second experience with Baba is that my youngest son was a bit weak in studies. That worried me and I always said Baba with tears in my eyes that why don't you give him knowledge and help him succeed in his life ?

I have read in Sai satcharitra that if you want to to get something fulfilled, you have to give up your most lovable thing. I normally loved two things very much one was non-veg and the other was Panipuri I couldn't give up non-veg because everyone in my in laws will get to know it and it won't have resulted anything. I decided to give up panipuri.

I left it nearly about four years. Once I had been to Shirdi when my son hasn't appeared his boards. while seeing a panipuri stall I couldn't resist myself but to my utter surprise I couldn't eat panipuri. Every time I went near the vendor he used to have some or the other problem. I got irritated and came back.

When his 10th boards were completed I went to Shirdi again and then I wished to eat pani puri because I got to know that he has passed with good marks. When I was about to eat panipuri my husband was calling me repeatedly but I couldn't receive his call. When I came back to my room and I called him, he said that that he got our son's certificate delivered in our home.

This proved that baba didn't want me to go against what I have promised him.

He is omnipresent and takes care of everything.

Omm sai ram
RAJASHREE MISHRA
BHUBANESWAR, ODISHA

BOW TO SHREE SAI, PEACE BE TO ALL

SAI -
A GLITTER TO ALL GLOOM

1. When I was in class 9th or 10th an old man came to our house and asked us to feed him with some food, thank God luckily we had some food left that day which will feed a personhappily.

He ate the food and went out of our Gate. My mother said me "go and call him and let us give him some bedsheets and dresses, I think he must not be having, he seems to be very poor "but when I went out and I searched for him I couldn't find him. I thought he must have gone to someone else's house and will be returning soon but even if waiting for 30 minutes I couldn't see him again in our locality.

From that particular day we got rid of various problems and tensions which we were facing.

When I and my husband were committed our families didn't get convinced because it was an inter-caste marriage. I prayed Baba a lot and said him that if you make both of us together then I will feed the poor people sitting out of your temple.

And then miraculously my in-laws agreed and said us from their side to take are relationship ahead and everything happened successfully. we are happily married and settled now.

I would like to thank Baba a lot he has been a strong pillar in every situation of my life I can't imagine my life without him.

Omm Sai Ram
SWETA ROUT DASH
GERMANY

BOW TO SHREE SAI, PEACE BE TO ALL

BABA - KING OF MAGICS

Experiences with Baba can't be noted down with Limitedwords.

I visited Shirdi in 2019 with my husband my sister and my family members. One morning we got ready for Nashik to get a Darshan in Shani Shingnapur and Trimbakeshwar. After returning to Shirdi all were very tired and didn't wished to you have a darshan of Baba but I was very curious and didn't want a day to get wasted without having a darshan of him. So I went alone I was afraid that it was getting late and if I could get a Darshan or not. When I went in, I saw that the temple was so empty that there were only 30 to 40 people inside the hall. I can't express that happiness I felt.

Another experiences was, I got a call from KV 2 Bhubaneswar to join but I denied.

After denying I felt guilty because they offered me a good salary. I felt really bad and I asked Baba that if if I had to join then why didn't you say me or why didn't you stop me from denying them and I send you that if you are really there then I will join the same school definitely and surprisingly I got a call from them again during the middle of November and I was called to join in the first week of December. The day I joined was Thursday so I am very grateful to Baba for making this possible and hearing to each and every pleading of mine.

Once we went to Manali while returning to Shimla the cab through which we went, I forgot my mobile phone in the cab This made all of us worry. I went to the Manali police station but that didn't help me in any way when we were just returning from the police station chanting Baba's name repeatedly and was requesting him to do any such kind of miracle which will give me back my phone. Suddenly when we saw forward the cab driver with whom we returned was standing in front of us.

We were completely surprised when we asked him about this, he didn't even know that my phone was still there in a car. My husband went with him and brought my phone which was there at the same place where I had kept.

I would like to say that a vote of thanks isn't enough for the one who knows everyone's pain and is ready to help every person who needs him.

Omm Sai Ram
Sushreeta Pradhan
BHUBANESHWAR,ODISHA

BOW TO SHREE SAI, PEACE BE TO ALL

SAI REPLCED MY FATHER WITH HIMSELF

After the death of my father, I was shattered, and was broken like anything. I only had my mother and sister with me at that time. One night I cried remembering my father. That night itself Sai baba came in my dreams and said me "don't worry my child, stay strong", he gave me a rose and said, "I am always there with you". That experience completely surprised me.

Just few days after it, I got my job and then my marriage was also successfully over.

After some days of our marriage my husband left his job. To do a business he was finding a suitable house but he couldn't.

I started doing 5 Sai Guruwar brat. And astonishingly my husband could find a house in just the completion of 2 guruwar only. I felt to happy and since then I believe that baba is always there with the one who searches him.

Omm sai Ram
LORISH ROUT
CUTTACK, ODISHA

BOW TO SHREE SAI, PEACE BE TO ALL

BABA -
A LIVING POWER

1. Baba is the living power I have ever felt. I went to nashik for some work 3 years a go and traveling from odisha to so nearest place of shiridi i just wanted a chance to go to my baba my pain healer.I was praying him to give me one chance for a esteemedmeet.

I went nashik with with my husband's elder brother and in odia culture we stay up with proper decorum even we don't pass things hand to hand. So I was bit confused if he will say yes to go shirdi and with hing nervousness and hope I asked him if we can go or not and its baba's blessing he said yes.

The next day we had our return flight at evening and we planned we will go there early morning and come back so we started at 4:30am and we reached at 5:45 am and unfortunately that day the Darshan time was closed upto 4: 00 pm and we had no time in hand to wait upto 4.I was too upset and I was praying hard for a miracle and suddenly I heard from someone that Darshan is available for 10mins only for pravat arti and I got a sparkle I was about to run but I got Spain I couldn't walk and the gate was closing in front of me I couldn't resist that I cried and it was really a miracle that my brother in law pulled me up and pushed me towards the gate and he too ran after me I was astonished because respecting the rules we have never even had a direct conversation but I thankfully was inside the temple and the gate closed just after us.He comforted me a bit saying not to worry am your elder brother I can't see you loosing hope.I was happy I got a chance to see my baba and also the fear I had for my brother in law since 18years was vanished.we were there in the temple for 1hr till the arti got over and me being short in height was struggling to get arti and then a police officer took me too close to baba's feet I got goosebumps and I got a flower from his feet which is with me now also.

Since that day the love and trust on baba has touched the sky limits.

Its my feelings I can just feel it but this book is giving me a chance to express it to the world a huge thanks for that.

Omm sai ram
SASMITA PANDA
BHUBANESHWAR, ODISHA

BOW TO SHREE SAI, PEACE BE TO ALL

SAI MAKES EVERY IMPOSSIBLE POSSIBLE

What to say about baba, I wake up seeing him and close my eyes seeing hispicture.

I used to worship him since a long time but the moment when I could realize his miracle was when he took me out from one of a deadly disease.

One day after regular uneasiness, I went through several tests. After the test reports came my husband took me to the Oncology department of Aiims Bhubaneshwar. I didn't know even what Oncology means. When I got to know that I was suffering from Cancer, I was completely devastated.

I just asked Baba that how could you give me such a big disease ? What mistake I did in your worship ?

I was so much scared for the FNAC test that I kept on chanting baba's name and I couldn't even realize a bit of pain. While returning home that day, I couldn't control my emotions and broke down into tears while saying my husband to take care of my daughter if anything happens to me. We both were in tears and that day was the most painful day in my life.

You would be surprised that each treatment of mine starting from the operation to the chemo therapy to the radiation therapy, I never lost my hope because I knew baba is always there with me.

I feel so blessed that Baba saved from everything, I always apply baba's Udi in my forehead which makes me feel that he is always with me.

So, all I wanted to say is, he is definitely there.

Om Sai Ram
REENA RAM
CUTTACK, ODISHA

BOW TO SHREE SAI, PEACE BE TO ALL

SAI - A REAL POWER EXISTING WITH ALL TRANSPARENCY

I never believed on a single God. I always used pray God as a whole and believed in my work. It was 2013 when Amy father faced a huge road accident. The situation was so bad that we had no hopes left with us.

He was without his senses for nearly a week. The doctor said it can lead to comma if he doesn't get back his senses shortly. But By god's grace he got back to senses but again he couldn't speak anything for because the vocal chord was severely affected. That again made us worried. Kept on praying baba which was the only thing I could do. Then just within few days he started talking and everything came to our control. He is totally a normal person now, no one can say that we went through such pains by seeing him now.

This is all due to baba's blessings which I believe.

Omm Sai Ram.

SMRUTIMAYEE SWAIN

CUTTACK, ODISHA

BOW TO SHREE SAI, PEACE BE TO ALL

WHY AM I NOT A VIP

There are a lot of experiences with him, let me say youone.

In 2007, me and few of my colleagues with our principal mam went to Shirdi. When we reached there, we all were very excited to see baba for the 1st time. There are several entries to the mandir, we were very confused from where to get in. We finally got into the temple and was very happy, but suddenly I found that my mother in law and my elder son are missing. I couldn't find them in that crowd. That made all of us worried. We couldn't even get back in the queue to search them. I kept on walking and finally a division came where there was a VIP lane and a normal lane. It was baba's arti time so the normal darshan was closed. I asked one lady in that queue who was from shirdi, that can I get a darshan of baba from this way, she said me, "only VIPs can go through this way", I thought that why am I not a VIP, atleast I could have got to see baba. Then to my utter surprise a lady called me to come and join her and not to say anything to anyone.

I went with her, I had tears in my eyes and felt that Baba himself called me.

Till then I forgot about my mother in law and son. When I came out after darshan, I felt panicked and started calling baba again, and just the moment I turned my head, I saw them standing right Infront of me.

I was so happy and elated that I can't forget that day ever in my life.

Baba has always been there with me. My younger son suffered from fits and I started doing 5 guruwar brat of baba then after that day I never say my son suffering from it even once. I always make a visit to Shirdi during Dushera and doesn't matter if we have enough finances with us or not but everything happens automatically and we visit him every year without failure

So I am always grateful to baba for his immense blessings and support.

Omm Sai Ram
DEBASHREE ROUT
CUTTACK, ODISHA

BOW TO SHREE SAI, PEACE BE TO ALL

THE GOD WITH VARIOUS INCARNATIONS - SAI

When I was traveling with my husband and my son on a late winter night, the fuel of our vehicle ran out. There wasn't even a single vehicle or person passing by. We were completely helpless and were trying to find out solution. I started praying Baba and seeking his help. All of sudden, a man in his scooter came and offered help. My husband was hesitant but the man persuaded him. He provided petrol from his own scooter, didn't accept a single penny and left before we could show our gratitude. I believe, he was no less than Sai Baba's incarnation.

Omm sai ram
LOPAMUDRA PATTANAIK
DELHI

BOW TO SHREE SAI, PEACE BE TO ALL

PATIENCE - A SOLUTION TO EVERY PAIN

What shall I say about baba's experiences, I just pray that everyone get a place under the tree of his blessings.

Since when I got to know about baba, I always had a desire of going to Shirdi. Once my husband made tickets of it but unfortunately I was had to go through a major surgery and couldn't visit. Rather my younger daughter went through my ticket.

I felt very sad and left it on him that whenever he wishes, I will go then.

One day on a family function, my elder daughter's father in law asked me, do you want to go with us ? We are going to Shirdi.

I can't express how elated and excited I was for visit baba's place for the 1st time.

We went and we did the darshan very well.

Life is all about ups and downs, I keep on asking a lot of questions to baba and to my utter surprise, I used to get every answer from the serial "Mo Sai" telecasted in Prarthana channel.

One day was so gloomy that I asked baba how to handle all pains at once baba ? How to get much strength ?

When I oned the TV and started watch the show "Mo sai" the moral baba gave in that episode was, "We should learn to have patience, "The only solution to everything is patience.

I feel baba's presence in every single day and in each during every hills and valleys that comes in my life.

Omm Sai Ram
LATIKA MOHANTY
CUTTACK, ODISHA

BOW TO SHREE SAI, PEACE BE TO ALL

UDI –
A MEDICINE TO ALL DISEASES

Sai baba has a miraculous healing power. My daughter was in class 5. He started suffering from a rare infection. We tried out many medications but nothing worked out. We used change several doctors and get her treated the way the doctors prescribed but we couldn't find any noticeable changes inher.

I felt helpless at a moment and started worship baba. I applied baba's udi on her body.

And the suddenly recovery we noticed can't be described in words. We felt very much grateful to baba. There isn't any end to his miraculous deeds. He plays a very vital role in my everyday's life.

I am thankful to him for everything.

Omm sai Ram

JAGRUTI PATTANAIK

CUTTACK, ODISHA

BOW TO SHREE SAI, PEACE BE TO ALL

BABA – A TREASURE OF HAPPINESS

Words will fall short to express baba'smiracles.

His deeds are always unbelievable. Once I did 9 Sai guruwar brat.

On the 9th thursday I went to the nearby temple to do the final worshipping to end my brat. I had also wished to feed some homeless people for which I had prepared some food and had taken with me. After doing the puja when I came out of the temple there was no one such whom I can feed.

I felt very disappointed and remembered if I had committed any mistakes while the puja. I was about to leave, then 5 little children came to me, I don't know from where they were and said me that they are very hungry and want some food to eat. I was so elated that tears of happiness rolled down from my eyes.

I couldn't express that feeling in words. I took out all the food I took with me and fed them well. Their happy faces made me feel that my brat is successful now.

Omm sai ram
SANJEETA PRATIHAR
CUTTACK, ODISHA

BOW TO SHREE SAI, PEACE BE TO ALL

THE CREATOR OF DEVOTION - SAI

Last time when I went to Shirdi, I was sitting in dwarka mai and was crying with bowed head,

Just thinking about when will I come next and a nostalgic feeling was hitting me hard. Then suddenly what happened was a chaddar (a piece of cloth) came and fell on me covering me. It was a winter night nearly about 1pm. The fan was off, there wasn't a blow of wind even. Everyone was surprised that from where did it came. A tall man who was standing near the door came towards me and said it's mine. I gave it to him. Then a pandit from there came and said me, don't cry sitting over here dear, Baba doesn't likes it.

Don't worry all your pain is taken by baba now. He will protect you and your family from everything which he showed you now by covering you with that chaddar.

Then another thing which happened was that when I got to know about an aunty who was a neighbor to us that she was suffering from a disease and all were thinking that it would be cancer, I felt really bad and cancer had no treatment then so I thought I will do worship baba by doing 5 guruwar brat. I started doing it. I tried giving all my efforts in making it as perfect as possible. In return I asked god to give me a little hint that he is present by being visible in any such way possible. At the end of the 1st guruwar, I was a bit disappointed that why I couldn't find anything such. I clicked pictures of baba and posted as my status.

One of my friends said me after looking at the pic that see baba is looking down, and that waw clearly visible in that picture. But when we went to see baba's idol, it was normal and he was looking up.

This was the heart warming moment in my life.

He is always there with everyone.

Omm sai ram
MADHUSMITA PATRA
CUTTACK, ODISHA

BOW TO SHREE SAI, PEACE BE TO ALL

BABA –
THE BIGGEST ASSET IN LIFE

So my first experience is how I came to know Satcharitra book.In 2015 I was working in Goa while in middle some thing went wrong with my husband and my relationship so once in office I got very sad and cried a lot at that time my office colleague Suvarna advice me to read Sai Satcharitra and I listened to her and started reading and within 8 days everything got solved and again we started happylife.

My second experience same year I though my mind Baba let me get a job in Pune of Salary 20000 moment next day I receive a call I interviewed on a phone and got a job in Pune for salary not 20k but 18k which I was Satisfied.

My third experience in June 2018 my husband was lost a job of professor for engineering college which he worked for 10 years and same time I got infected for tuberculosis I felt again sad again I started reading Satcharitra finished 2 times within 15 days my husband got a job and I too cured within 2 months.

Another experience some in July 2020 I got a dream in that dream my daughter was playing on a bridge and she slips in water I cried a lot a suddenly I saw Sai baba giving a blessing (he saved my child from all dangers) and next day I saw a msg of Seetha Sis like who is interested in reading satcharithra daily pranayanam. As if Baba himself advice me to read Satcharitra daily pranayanam

I was not having issue from 6 years so same year Dec 2018 I got pregnant and my husband got a offer for good company with good package and August 2019 I blessed with a daughter

Recently 8 days before one man with Goddess came to my house and asked my For money I said him my husband is not at home u please come another day he Force me and said I am not asking much but only 205 rs so I checked my purse and exactly I was having 200 and 5 Rs dollar and I remember of Sai baba again and gave him.

One small experience I was pregnant on, 8 month I thought as my delivery is little complicated so I wish I would get a Udi of Baba in evening my brother not knowing anything my brother come and give me a udi and I was surprised.

Omm Sai Ram
HARSHANA VINAYAK JADHAV
PUNE

BOW TO SHREE SAI, PEACE BE TO ALL

SAI - THE STRONGEST SUPPORT SYSTEM

There are innumerable blessings from sai in my life. I feel without him I wouldn't be able to live this life. He was and is always with me and he proved it from time to time.. Even he comes in various form to pass this message tome...

Sharing the recent blessing of baba..

I was travelling from Mumbai to Bhubaneswar and while coming to my home i lost my wallet somewhere. I had all my credit debit cards, all my original ID proofs in it. I was so tensed to notice that I came home after a year... I couldn't sleep well, eat well. I prayed baba to please get my wallet because I had my Papa's coins which he gave me during my graduation, my nani's note which I kept since 1 year. Today when my mom went office, an auto driver came searching for her and delivered my purse. He said he was searching since last night and finally found. I believe that auto driver was my baba who handed over my purse safely with all documents in it. Thank you my baba I know you are always there for me... Thank you baba for listening to my prayers always.. Thank you baba for teaching me the path of shraddha saburi. Please be with me and my family always..

Anant Koti Bramhand Nayak Rajadhiraja Yogiraja Sadhguru SaiNath Maharaj Ki Jai..

Omm sai ram

SELVY DAS

PUNE

BOW TO SHREE SAI, PEACE BE TO ALL

NEEM LEAF - A TASTE OF HAPPINESS

My love for sai baba is always unsaid and beyond the world. My experience with him is very evident. I went to Shirdi for the 1st time with my whole family in 2011. I was very happy and ecstatic. We all visited the mandir and the darshan went very well. After that went near the neem tree for the pradakshana and its considered to be very auspicious to find a neem leaf from the tree. I was the lucky one to find aleaf.

The next time I want shirdi was on April 2019 after my marriage with my husband and my inlaws. As usual we did the darshan and went near the Neem tree, and holla! Once again I found a leaf there. And a white rose fell onto my head while I was asking Baba to bless me with a child. And guess what ! I conceived in the month of May after being failure thrice. Isn't this a miracle ?

Baba's leela can't be expressed in words. He is omnipresent and holds immense powers within him.

Omm sai Ram

SHRADHA PARIDA

DELHI

BOW TO SHREE SAI, PEACE BE TO ALL

TRUE DEVOTION CAN CHANGE ANYTHING

1. What shall I say about baba ? Whenever I take his name, I get some invisible positive energy and confidence. When I chant Shirdi Sai baba's gayatri mantra, every obstacles move far away. Although I have a lot of memories connected with baba, I would like to shareone.

Once my daughter got very very high fever. At that time we couldn't take any other decision than admitting her in the hospital. We consulted our doctor and he said to admit her because she had 105 temperatures. But I knew she would be alright as baba is with us.

So finally we packed our bags and went to the hospital. The room was already booked by one of our relative.

While going I thought we should go to baba's temple which is near by first before going to hospital. I couldn't stop my tears when I started expressing my pain to baba.

There my daughter asked his father for a hundred rupees and she put that in the donation box. I was s surprised that how can a 4 years old child can think of doing such. I thought may be she too has some feelings for baba.

Then when we went to the hospital and consulted our regular doctor he said that your daughter's condition is alright now and no need to admit her. If the temperature changes you can consult me. Then suddenly some tears came into my eyes, when this unbelievable incident happened with us.

Baba's blessings are always with the one who can feel it.

Omm Sai Ram
SUMITRA BHUYAN
CUTTACK, ODISHA

BOW TO SHREE SAI, PEACE BE TO ALL

INNER PEACE IS EVERYTHING

It's near about 10years back, I didn't believe in Baba, I heard about him a lot from one of my colleagues. He had a strong faith in baba, once he had given me an old Sai Parayana book and said go through it at least once you may feel good but I only kept that book with me and never read a single page. Unexpectedly my father faced cardiac problems that time we all become panic, that time I started reading Sai Parayana book and miracle happened, my father got cure from all, and from that time I feel like I am my Sai Baba's child. I need baba's presence every time in my life, I don't know how and why I feel so but gradually I started talking with him in my inner sense in everymoment.

Secondly, when I got married I suffered a lot but that time didn't bring my book with me even I forget to recall my baba because so many disturbances were there in my in-law's house, I felt like some back magics are also applying for me, I started getting disconnected with all the faith on God, never wondering to visit the temple even if started self-injury activities, which is unbelievable because I'm not like that type. I discussed all these things in my family but initially, no one believed me, but after I spent some time with my family in my home also same things were going on. Then my parents suggested me to take sai baba's book with me so I did the same, and surprisingly all things were normalized. I could feel a peace. I still survive only because of my baba, he escaped me from my bad experiences and always givea me the courage to live my life. My baba makes me understand inner peace is everything, doesn't matter if we have anything with us or not but we should have the trust and power to get everything.

I'm still alive, my family members are safe including me and I'm self-independent only because of my baba.

Omm Sai Ram
SMITA MOHANTY
CUTTACK, ODISHA

BOW TO SHREE SAI, PEACE BE TO ALL

BABA -A LISTENER TO ALL PLEADINGS

I have numerous memories with baba, each step I take forward, I couldn't feel his presence in mylife.

He has taken from nothing to everything. I love singing his songs and whenever get an opportunity for baba's shows,doesn't matter how busy I am, I always make sure I attend it.

Starting from getting selected in the auditions to being a RJ in FM Rainbow, he has always been with me.

When I fell in love with my husband, none of our families were convinced for our marriage, since he was an odia and I was bengali. So I always prayed baba and requested him to make this possible. And fortunately he did this and we are happily married now.

While my daughter was about be delivered, my condition deteriorated, because my umbilical cord got wrapped around her and that was a difficult situation. But due baba's blessings my daughter got delivered safely and we were healthy at the same time.

Although expressing gratitude to him is impossible, I would like to say that I am always indebted to him.

Omm Sai Ram

SIULI GHOSH

CUTTACK, ODISHA

BOW TO SHREE SAI, PEACE BE TO ALL

BABA AND HIS UDI – THE BEST COMBINATION

When I was in class 6th, I went through the appendicitis operation. I was denied to eat any kind of junk foods and drink plenty of water. I couldn't make a habit of drinking morewater.

Once when I went to my aunty's home, I felt a severe pain in my stomach.

My aunty used to pray Sai baba a lot and was a true believer of baba's blessings. She brought baba's Udi and put it on my stomach and on my forehead.

And within a hour the pain was relieved and I felt good. Since then I could find a miraculous power in baba and started worshiping him.

I believe whoever calls baba with love and devotion, baba definitely listens to them.

Omm sai ram
MOUSUMI MOHANTY
CUTTACK, ODISHA

BOW TO SHREE SAI, PEACE BE TO ALL

SAI - A SAVIOR FROM ALL EVIL POWERS

When Baba came into my life he changed me into a down to earth person. He completed transformed mypersonality.

I started believing baba long back when very less people knew him.

I always prayed baba to bless me with a son.

And after praying him for years together, we were blessed with a son after 13 years of our marriage.

I cannot thank much to him for this. This will always remain in everyone's heart forever.

Another day when I was returning home at night some people who we against me started attacking me and I couldn't understand how I could get escaped from that situation. I chanted baba's name repeatedly and thankfully I came home safely and nothing happened to me.

Later I got to know that the photo of baba which was being worshipped in the khannagar temple started burning at the particular time when I was facing that situation.

So I felt like baba took that thing upon him and saved me.

Omm Sai Ram

PRASANTA PATRA

CUTTACK, ODISHA

BOW TO SHREE, PEACE BE TO ALL

61

SAI - THE BIGGEST PROBLEM SOLVER

There are always a invisible power in our faith and this supreme power always protects us in our lives from every difficulties. I have so many experiences with my baba but among those I have a most special experience which I can't never forget. Here I would like to share that incident with all of you, which was a miracle forme.

I still remember that day was 14th Jan 2010 a Thursday. A group of Sai devotees just went by our house and one of them came to our home and he said that he wanted to have a glass of water to drink. Then he was sitting with us started talking about so many things about us which really made us surprised then he suddenly told me that you are going to get married soon and that time I was doing Post Graduation in Psychology at Ravenshaw University.

That time we didn't believe him. I thought he just tried to manipulate us. Then I asked him about my in-laws family just for fun because at that time I couldn't even think about my marriage. Then my mother offered him a cup of tea and at that time I asked him about my carrier after marriage then he replied with a smile "Don't try to drink a cup of tea at a time, otherwise your mouth will burn." But then I couldn't 9understand his version. Then he left us with his blessings. That day was a Thursday and we had a plan to went Purighat Sai Baba's temple. When we were reached at the temple, Baba's Arti was just stopped that time and we were standing in a queue to see baba. But it was really a miracle which happened with me that when I reached near baba, the Pandit ji removed a mala from Baba and offered me that. I was shocked. I didn't have any words to say. And you won't believe that, this was the incident on January and I was getting married on March. And my life still going on as his every version.

I always surrender my life to my Baba. I know he is always with me when no one is for me.

Omm Sai Ram
SWATI MOHANTY
CUTTACK, ODISHA

BOW TO SHREE SAI, PEACE BE TO ALL

I LOVE YOU BABA

We all know that Sai baba knows a everything. He fulfills all wishes of his devotees. I have a sweet experience withhim.

One day we were in shirdi, we went to the temple to see baba. We went to see baba's aarti which was just going to start. But we got stuck in a queue for hours. When the queue started moving ahead we moved inside. But again there came another queue and we waited for hours. When we entered we saw that the entrance gate had been closed. We were very sad. But after 15 minutes the entrance gate opened and we went inside. Me and father got separated from my mother in two different queues. The hall was full with people. Surprisingly a small place was there which is for one person only. My mother went and sat down there. She called me and I went and sat on her lap. The aarti was going on in front of us. We saw it clearly and happily.

Sai baba looked very cute.

I love you baba..

Omm Sai Ram

INDEE PATTANAIK

CLASS - 3 STUDENT

CUTTACK,ODISHA

BOW TO SHREE SAI, PEACE BE TO ALL

BABA- A CONSTANT THROUGHOUT MY LIFE

When it comes towards baba I am completelyspeechless.

'Baba the name only suggests purity and peace". I connect to him in every stages of my life.

I am student, not so good at studies nor in anything. I really and personally don't like myself, why I don't know. From class 6 to class 10, I only scored nearly about 60-70 %. I really try best but I never got the results. I broke every minute, every day.

Once I cried a lot and called baba, and asked "why you brought me to this world. I am not good at anything. I have lost faith in myself."

But sitting in silent position in a closed room when I cried that then I felt like baba came and said me in my mind, "Child everyone Is a gift of god. Everyone is the product of nature. You have something special with you. But you can't see that. Tell your family about your weakness."

Only after that thing I scored 88% in class 10th.

I mostly do baba's prayers everyday and baba's fasting on thursdays.

Once in class 12th when I was going to appear the board exam, I went to baba's temple. That day we had physics and

I didn't study one chapter and had to skip it but surprisingly only one easy question came from that chapter and the 2 difficult questions in the paper were the ones I practiced the day before. I was so amazed. And my happiness knew no limits when I got 93% in boards.

From that day I have a great belief in baba.

Omm sai ram
ADITI MOHANTY
CUTTACK, ODISHA

BOW TO SHREE SAI, PEACE BE TO ALL

HIS BLESSINGS A KEY TO EVERY SUCCESS

I believe that, the one who could feel baba is the one who could achieve hisblessings.

When I was asked to share some experiences with Baba I was a bit puzzled because he is himself the god of experiences. The one who has tried to feel him is the one who could get him.

This is an incident of 2008 or 2009 when I was working in Doordarshan as a programming director at that time Technology wasn't that developed. One day when I completed the shooting and editing and when I was about to transfer I couldn't do it. I don't know what problem happened but including my Studio I roamed about 10 to 12 more studios in Cuttack and Bhubaneswar but still I wasn't able to do it.

It had to be telecasted on 8:15 a.m. on the next day so I had to do it anyhow at that moment. It was 8 o'clock and I was returning from Cuttack to Bhubaneswar. On the way I got a message in my mobile phone but I ignored it and came to my studio and started working again. Everything sorted out well and I could complete my work within few minutes. I transferred it to Doordarshan and deposited there.

I couldn't understand that the work for which I was trying for the whole day how can it be complete in just few minutes. When my work was over I came out and went a near by tea stall. When I was having my tea during that time I opened my phone and checked what that message was.

The message was from an elder brother as well as a singer Mr Sudhakar Mishra.

It was written in the message that

"Baba saw you are in trouble and facing problems now everything will be alright Baba's blessing is with you ".

I was completely amazed and I started reminding and I found out that only after I got the message I was successful in completing my work.

Not only once or twice but three times my ticket to Shirdi was cancelled. I couldn't visit Baba and when I got a chance to go, I did Baba's Darshan which felt like it was a blessing to me and I couldn't believe my eyes that I was seeing Baba directly through my eyes. Tears of happiness roll down my cheeks when one of my brother asked me why are you crying ?

I said no I am not crying this is just a feeling for Baba because he is the god of feelings and the one who could feel baba is the one who could achieve his blessings.

Omm Sai Ram

SARALA PRASAD MISHRA

CUTTACK, ODISHA

BOW TO SHREE SAI, PEACE BE TO ALL

THE ONLY RAY OF HOPE IN THE DARKNESS

From the day I started worshipping baba I got sure that my family is in safe hands recently I faced a very tragic incident in mylife.

Due to some personal issues the owner of the house where we were staying asked us to leave the home as soon as possible, the time was nearly about 11 o'clock in night. I couldn't understand that how will I take all our belongings with my family to a new place that to in this dark night.

I had no other options than leaving the house at that particular moment. I prayed Baba a lot.

I said him you are the only one who can help us my wife was praying vigorously and was chanting his name repeatedly.

Then just within few minutes a person who is very close to us who stayed just nearby came to our house and asked uswhat happened. We we said the situation, he said

"come with me,I have one room vacant and in my house, you can accommodate there until you get a new house".

I felt that it was Baba himself who helped us in that very tragic situation and helped us to get a safe shelter at that dark night.

Omm Sai Ram

MANOJ KUMAR MOHANTY

CUTTACK, ODISHA

BOW TO SHREE SAI, PEACE BE TO ALL

71

A CONNECTION WITH BABA TO BE ADORED

I have never seen someone believing in god so much. It was for the first time I realised that people are so much connected with Sai Baba. During my college days when I was staying in a PG with one of my friend named Arpita this incident happened withme.

When the owner of the house instructed us to take all the things out from my room because the room was to be coloured we took all the things out but she had pasted a picture of Sai Baba in the wall of the room, when the owner said to take it out she didn't accept it.

She said that if I take that picture out it will tear into pieces so let that picture be pasted on the wall but the owner didn't agree, so she cried a lot and finally the picture was taken out from the wall and nothing happened to that picture it was completely same as before.

We all were surprised, then she said that it is the power of Baba. To the one he loves, he never betrays them. I was completely astonished to see such connection of people with Lord sai.

Omm Sai Ram

SAJITA MOHANTY
CUTTACK, ODISHA

BOW TO SHREE SAI, PEACE BE TO ALL

A MIRACLE OUT OF EXPECTATIONS

I have always heard about Baba's exceptional miracles from people. From the day started worshipping him I found, he stands with us as a pillar in all our ups anddowns.

In the year 2013, one day I was roaming in the verendah of our house, I found a neem leaf. Although there isn't even a single neem leaf near our house I was completely surprised I felt like tasting the leaf, when I tasted the leaf it was sweet in taste and we all were completely amazed that how can this be possible and from where did this leaf come from.

I called one of our relatives who is a very big devotee of Baba. He said me that Baba has blessed your family through this leaf and since thet day, we started worshipping Baba seriously and every thursday we conduct his Pujas in a very particular way.

He comes to people in different incarnations, he helps everyone in different forms in different ways but he always returns the real result of what we do.

Omm Sai Ram
GITANJALI PATTANAIK
KALAHANDI, ODISHA

BOW TO SHREE SAI, PEACE BE TO ALL

HIS DEEDS A MAGNETIC FORCE

Belonging to the Jagannath Dham Puri I had never thought of getting sheltered under the devotional tree of Sai Baba. When I got married, my in-laws were true devotees of Baba, so after my marriage from 2011 we used to visit Shirdi every year, but I never had a feeling of devotion for baba I just used to go as a trip and come back again but when I faced lot of problems in my life during 2014 to 2016, I gained a believe and faith in myself for Baba.

When in 2017 I visited Shirdi, I said Baba if you

are really there then you will let me see your aarti because it is highly discussed among people and everyone loves it,so I too want to see it please make it possible.

I got a bit late, so when I reached the gates were already closed and when aarti starts, each time you have to stay there for at least 1 hour. Neither you can move forward nor you can move backward. So I was stuck there, I was praying Baba hard, I was very upset but suddenly what happened was a police who was standing over there opened the gate in front of me and I was after 15 to 20 people and he said we can leave 20 to 25 people from this queue, so come on.

Everyone started running and I too started running with them then just after few minutes,

I was standing in front of Baba watching his aarti. What can be more special than this ?

Omm Sai Ram

SANGHAMITRA SAHOO

CUTTACK, ODISHA

BOW TO SHREE SAI, PEACE BE TO ALL

BABA -
A GREAT MIND READER

Like some devotees I don't have a habit of going to the temple of Baba regularly but sometimes I visit a small temple situated near my house. One day I don't know what happened to me but an internal desire came to me when I saw Baba that day in the temple. I just wanted to visit Shirdi I didn't know how it can be possible but I prayed baba and requested him to make this possible. At that Temple a dog sits in a particular place every time. I was sitting on the steps of the temple and that dog suddenly came and licked myfingers.

I was surprised that why did he do that then I got a call, when I checked, it was from the Sun of one of my very intimate friends. He said me that uncle we are planning to go to Shirdi will you join us ? I said ofcourse why are you asking me I was just thinking of it now.

That day I could realise the potential of Baba and up to what extent he listens to his devotees being an 80 year old person I had a safe journey with my wife and people took good care of mine.

The second time I felt Baba close to me was when I was willing to get a neem leaf from the neem tree which I have heard tastes sweet.

The entire place was clean, when I was returning back with a disappointed face, a sweeper of the temple in his uniform called me from back asked me "do you want a leaf ?" I said," yes I want ". He gave me a leaf and then again I felt grateful to Baba.

Omm Sai Ram
Dr. GIRIJA PRASAD ACHARYA
BHUBANESHWAR, ODISHA

BOW TO SHREE SAI, PEACE BE TO ALL

AARTI –
AN ETERNAL PEACE

When I was at an young age I wished to make a temple at khannagar of Cuttack. I and two to three brothers of mine started keeping a picture of Baba and started doing Aarti. We used to do the 4 aarti of baba everyday. We always had a dream of making a temple over there. It took us two years of time, many people said many things we went through a lot of difficulties but finally a beautiful temple could stand strong at that place and that was only possible because of Baba. Not only this we are able to conduct prashad seban on every thrusday for more than 2000people.

Onece when I visited Shirdi, one pandit of baba's samadhi temple is quite close to me, when I called him he said me, "come through the queue to Dwarka mai I am there inside you can watch the aarti from there" but I said "I don't want to watch the Aarti, I want to do it myself "so he said me okay its alright, when I came out of the temple he sent a person to me who took me to a place named Sai Dham, 20 kilometers far from sai temple. Baba used to sit there.

When I reach there it was the time of Madhyan Aarti. I did the complete aarti by my own and I felt so good when I realized that Baba heard my inner voice.

I felt really blessed and touched.

Omm Sai Ram

BASANT KUMAR JENA

CUTTACK, ODISHA

BOW TO SHREE SAI, PEACE BE TO ALL

SAI - THE LORD OF UNIVERSE

Attachment with Baba was when I started visiting the khannagar Sai Temple regularly. One day in the afternoon I was sleeping, I saw a dream, that suddenly it started raining and the rain water came inside our house and it destructed everything starting from the temples to everything so my family members got very worried and they were calling me and suddenly I woke up and then I realized that baba is with me, if we completely devote ourselves to him and dedicate our life to him then nothing can hamperus

Everyday I go to the temple for at least one Aarti but one day I asked that I always go to the temple at the time of you Aarti but you never gave me a single chance, for doing your aarti, day when I said this to Baba just the next day what happened was when I went to the temple, Pandit Ji who used to do the Aati was absent so my small brothers present over there called me that you come and do the aarti today and I can't express my feelings of that particular situation. I got Goosebumps and I started crying I was doing the aarti and tears were going on flowing from my eyes.I can't explain that situation.

Then I said to Baba that "baba you are to truthful, you are so much omnipresent, you can know everyone's pain at once ?

How can this be possible ? The answer was" he was the lord of Universe the greatest soul who carries within himself a power which can heal everything and anything ".

Omm Sai Ram

KARUNAKAR BARIK

CUTTACK, ODISHA

BOW TO SHREE SAI, PEACE BE TO ALL

SAI –
CALMNESS TO ALL STORMS

I came in contact with Baba in about 2014. My son suffered from asthma, so one of my friend said that you should start worshipping Baba, he will cure him and he will make everything alright. I started doing Sai gurubar brat. Eventually when I started worshipping him I marked he is making my life easier thanbefore.

I always had a desire to visit Shirdi but it was very difficult to convince my husband once when he came from his tour he said me from his side that I was thinking of visiting Shirdi, let's go once I was very much surprised that how can this be possible, so we finally made our tickets for Shirdi.

The day we had to go, we found that only one ticket was confirmed from three, so you were confused that what should we do but I said let's go and lets leave it on Baba he will take care of it but out of surprise we found that when we just stepped into the train all the three tickets offer were confirmed.

This is all baba's miracles which I believe.

Omm Sai ram
SUSHREE SANGEETA ACHARYA
BHUBANESHWAR, ODISHA

BOW TO SHREE SAI, PEACE BE TO ALL

BABA - THE BIGGEST TEACHER

Although I don't have any particular experience with Baba but I have learnt numerous things in the process of worshippinghim.

To every single person who believes that he or she is a devotee of Baba or who has ever visited Baba's temple once then he knows that how important the two words 'Shradha' and 'saburi' are.

Baba doesn't believe in prolonged fasting or prolonged Puja for him but he believes in serving to mankind, he believes in helping others.

He says if you want to get my blessings then be cheerful, be helpful, be down to earth to the whole world, and in which incarnation I will come to you, you never know.

In his book Sai satcharitra it's written that we should always give up ego, jealousy and many such things which hinders us from leaving a positive lifestyle.

He is not only God who who spreads humanity and brotherhoodness and most importantly he teacher us to believe in our work rather than just teorshiping him.

He is not only the lord of Universe but the biggest teacher I have ever seen

Omm Sai Ram

SWARNAMAYEE MOHANTY

BHUBANESHWAR, ODISHA

BOW TO SHREE SAI, PEACE BE TO ALL

BABA- THE REAL PRESENCE OF GOD

I started worshipping Baba since my school days when I was in my college. My brother planned of visiting Shirdi with his wife, daughter and maternal family. I too had a desire to go but I didn't say him anything. One night when he was sleeping, the day before he was about to make the tickets, Baba came to his dream and said him "how can you come without bringing the biggest worshipper of me in your home, you have to bring her with me "my brother couldn't get it what baba was saying and when he asked Baba about whom you are saying, baba dragged my hand and he got a glimpse of me he suddenly came to me and said my father that I want to take her with me so finally I went with them to Shirdi.

I can't express my happiness.

I always say baba that help me but never come to me directly because I will definitely be scared while seeing directly.

The Hotel where we stayed had a big photo of baba hanged on the wall of the room. When I was just sitting on the bed and I look at the photo I felt like baba is saying something to me and I went subconscious and I started talking to baba.

The next day when we went to get a darshan of Baba after coming out from the hall we went do Mhalsapati's house where I found many belongings of Baba. I saw two dresses were hanging which Baba used to wear. I wished to touch it but when I put my hand inside the cover a lady who was sitting there who is a member of the corresponding generations of Baba, scolded me and said why are you touching it and at that particular moment a needle got inserted in her finger with which she was sewing something. Then she said me sorry and allowed me to touch baba's dress and hug it.

Next day when I again went to have a darshan of Baba when I was near Baba's samadhi I picked up a rose from there and I thought of bringing that with me. A Pandit shouted very loudly on me and said you can't take that and keep it from where you picked it up. I felt really bad I said "Baba why did you do that with me ?"

I got so insulted in front of so many people.

But then what happened was completely out of everyone's expectations the big Mala of flower which Baba was wearing just fell down suddenly. I returned back, when I was moving towards the exit Gate a security guard suddenly called me and said "listen, listen ! Pandit Ji is calling you "

when I went back near Baba's samadhi they give me the complete big flower Mala and I was so amazed and no surprise that I can't thank Baba much for this I don't know what kind of blessings he showed me in this way. Even today when I remember that moment, I get goosebumps.

Omm Sai Ram

MANDAKINEE MOHANTY

CUTTACK, ODISHA

BOW TO SHREE SAI, PEACE BE TO ALL

CUTTACK, ODISHA

BOW TO SHREE SAI, PEACE BE TO ALL

SHIRDI - A PLACE OF INTERNAL HAPPINESS

Sai - Sa - Sakhyat, i -ishwar

This devotee of Sai has dedicated himself near baba since the last 25 years for which I am highly grateful.

The Protector of the world and the one whom I have accepted as a family member to me. In every ups and downs and every good and bad I feel that he is always there in my side. From my experiences I will only say that I can't imagine a life in this world without Sai. In every place in every aspect of my life the thoughts and bhajans of him keep reciprocating in every breath of mine. When I think of experiences with him I truly get goosebumps.

As we all know 2020 was converted into a deadly year, on the day of Diwali that year we all decided to celebrate it in our home itself. I lighted some Dias near Baba since I have heard he used to light the Masjid and increased its alluring beauty.

I invited few friends of mine to join me and celebrate that festival. We all did Baba's aarti together and the main reason for the arrangement was to discuss one thing which was, when will the temple of Shirdi be opened for Darshan. Everyone was filled with huge expectations to see baba as soon as possible, and you won't believe that at that particular moment a call came to me from Shirdi which made us know that Baba's Darbar is going to open after 2 days from Diwali for everyone's Darshan. Happiness knew no limits I could feel the elation which reflected out as glitters in everyone face.

Omm Sai Ram
DILLIP KUMAR DAS
CUTTACK, ODISHA

BOW TO SHREE SAI, PEACE BE TO ALL

HE CANT SEE HIS DEVOTEES IN PAIN

Baba is the lord of universe to express his miraculous Divas in words is impossible for a layman like me.

As said by Baba, once you set your feet in shirdi you will forget all your pains and I have realised it myself.

Once I went to Shirdi with some renowned musicians, it was the occasion of Guru Purnima. There was a huge crowd it was very difficult to have a darshan of Baba just once a day but I used to get the Darshan since the last three days but I wasn't able to come in contact with Baba's Samadhi.

I was really sad about it and tried my best. We just had one day in our hand, on the last day of Darshan when I was just about to reach near baba and was at a distance of nearly two to three people, I could see that the samadhi is enclosed with net and glass wires. It highly disappointed me that I stayed there for four days but I couldn't get in contact with Baba's Samadhi but to my surprise, a person who was after me was holding Baba's chaddar and some Prasad. When he took all those and went near the samadhi, a security guard came and opened the samadhi. He pushed nearly about five of us inside and I could touch Baba and I can't express the feeling I had at that time. After coming out, in the televisions displayed, I saw that the samadhi was again closed, it was a agian covered with the glass wires and nets.

All I could say is, there isn't any end to Baba's miraculous powers and the only one who searches him and try to feel him is the one who could achieve his blessings.

Omm Sai Ram

AMRUT RANJAN DASH

CUTTACK, ODISHA

BOW TO SHREE SAI, PEACE BE TO ALL

A BEAUTIFUL INITIATIVE TAKEN FOR BABA

The centre of all attractions in the whole world rajadhiraj Sadguru Sainath Maharaj. Every movement of my life holds forgettable memories with LordSai.

In 2017 when I went to Shirdi I had a wish to see baba's Chavadi Yatra and surprisingly it happened that evening only and I got a chance to carry Baba's sedan (palinki) in my shoulder.

When that Yatra ended I decided that we the devotees of odisha will do a chavadi yatra in shirdi the coming year and informed baba. All preparations were started from month of may 2018. We decided that in the month of July we will have both Chavadi yatra and bhajan program.

We nearly about 80 people in the month of July travelled to Shirdi and arranged everything. To our utter surprise on that particular day 300 Odia Sai devotees got together and it turned out into a very big Yatra. Much more bigger than our expectations. The Yatra was completed successfully and peacefully, it was a very proud moment for every Odia.

In the same way in 2019 also we could conduct a same kind of a Yatra which was even bigger and it included about 450 odias.

We planned that in the year of 2020 the number of devotees will cross 1000 but unfortunately Corona hit the world hard and this can't be possible but this year that is in the year of 2021 we will will definitely make sure that we do it in a more bigger way. I would like to conclude with Baba's words "who comes forward with one step for me, I will move forward with 10 steps for him".

It is only Baba who makes everything possible and this can only be said by the one who has realised it.

Let's dedicate ourselves near Baba, with patience let's consider this world to be a family and with love and happiness let's say it loud

"Jay shree Sai"

Omm Sai Ram
ULLASH CHANDRA BEHURA
CUTTACK, ODISHA

BOW TO SHREE, PEACE BE TO ALL

HE HANDLES EVERYTHING

I am a small devotee of baba since 2006. I was actually thinking how to become a devotee of baba because the place where I belong to had two temples of Satya Sai and till then also I was unknown to shirdi Sai baba's powers.

I heard everything about him and gradually started baba's bhajan and programs. Gradually many people joined us.

I remember on diwali when the bhajans of baba was going on, I kept a diya and put some water to test of baba has paid a visit to that place or not but I observed for two minutes that the diya kept lighting even without oil. Gradually faith and belief kept on increasing on baba. I shared this with my family and friends.

Once I was on a trip to Shirdi with my friends. We started our journey from Jharsuguda railway station. I forgot to take my mobile charger and my phone got switched off. I tried a lot but couldn't switch on the phone. I could not inform my parents because I did not remember anyone's number from my family.

I must say it was a miracle because when we reached Kopargaon, the mobile was completely off but as a habit of making the mobile on when I pressed the switch button in the early morning, the mobile suddenly got on and I could see Baba's picture on the display of my mobile for two to three minutes. I felt like I got Baba.

Whenever I face any problem I feel like Baba gives out the solution of everything through his udi.

I remember when I was in Jammu my wife called me and said that she was feeling some pain in her stomach because the delivery date was approaching. I said her not to worry and pray Sai Baba. I advised her to take some Udi and go to the hospital with my parents.

When I was travelling back I got a news that I was blessed with a baby boy whom I named Sai Swaroop.

Omm Sai Ram
SURENDRA PRADHAN
JHARSUGUDA, ODISHA

BOW TO SHREE SAI, PEACE BE TO ALL

WE NEVER KNOW IN WHICH FORM HE ARRIVES

Its been a long time, I have been worshipping baba. I regularly do Sai guruwar brat. One day I was late from the morning and during the madhyan aarti, I got too late. I hurriedly prepared chappati and sabji, I was just about to start the aarti, I heard someone calling at the door steps. When I checked, it was an old man asking for some food to it. It was a hot summer afternoon. I got into a troublesome situation. I didn't cook anything else than what I had prepared for aarti, I was already late and at the same time if I don't give food to that man, he would leave too in that sunnyday.

So I took the food which I prepared for the aarti and gave it to him. He ate it happily and went away and I never saw him again.

Wasn't he baba himself ?

Once again when I thought of doing another sai guruwar brat, I thought that everything required for the puja is already there, I don't need to buy anything. Then at night nearly about 10 pm when I went to the puja room and checked, the aarti book was missing. I had to do the kakad aarti at 4am and it was already late till then. I went to sleep but I was unable. When I felt asleep, I saw a dream where a book seller is passing by our house and I was saying when we have a bunch of books Infront of us then why to worry. Then when I woke up and went to do the aarti, the book was there in the puja room.

Isn't this just more than a miracle.

Omm sai ram

GITANJALI BEURA

BHUBANESWAR

BOW TO SHREE SAI, PEACE BE TO ALL

BABA – A SHADOW BEHIND ME FOREVER

My link with baba is since the past 10-12 years. When we shifted from Bhubaneswar to Cuttack, we found a photo of Sai baba already present in the home where we got shifted in Cuttack. We started worshipping him.

During my class 10 boards one person gave me baba's jantra and said me to keep it will me till my exams are over. The examiners normally don't allow me to take that with me but I used to fight with them and take it anyhow with me.

So finally when I got my results, it was very good. This made be believe baba and his miraculous powers.

Then everything went well. I went to USA for the 1st time in my life and that to alone. I didn't know anything about it neither their systems nor their rules and regulations. I always prayed baba to guide me and bring me home back safely. And I felt like baba remained with me as a shadow and helped me every time I have searched him.

So baba is a family member to us. Whenever we have choose between things and we get puzzled, we toss both yes and no and go exactly with his decisions.

Baba has a superior power which has no explanations.

I am grateful I got a chance to share my experiences.

Omm Sai Ram

ANTARA CHAKRABORTY

CUTTACK, ODISHA

BOW TO SHREE SAI, PEACE BE TO ALL

HE WRAPS US WITH HIS WARMTH BLESSINGS

Once my son Raghav was very unwell. He suffered from stool infections. We tried out reaching many doctors but no medicines worked out. I went to khannagar Sai temple, the pandit gave me chaddar which he said to put below the head of my son while sleeping. I did that and I also give him Baba's udi. Fortunately he was alright within fewdays.

Sciences and technologies are apart but the blessings of god is apart which works like wonders.

When I was pregnant my doctor warned me that I have a very low placenta and I need to take bed rest for complete nine months but situation wasn't favorable to me. I had to go to the school. So what I did was that I applied some udi in my navel and went to the school till the nine month of my pregnancy.

So this is no less than a miracle to me. Baba is truly a constant support system. I am always grateful to him for his immense involvement in my life and his numerous offerings to me.

Omm sai ram
KOMAL WADHWA
CUTTACK, ODISHA

BOW TO SHREE SAI, PEACE BE TO ALL

LIST OF CONTRIBUTORS

- Each and every beautiful soul who shared their heart warming experiences.

- The reason behind this initiative, whose blessings made this book possible.

www.ingramcontent.com/pod-product-compliance
Lightning Source LLC
LaVergne TN
LVHW050416160726
843469LV00041B/1101